THE FLYING BEAVER BROTHERS AND THE EVIL PENGUIN PLAN

MAXWELL EATON III

ALFRED A. KNOPF
NEW YORK

THIS IS A BORZOI BOOK PUBLISHED BY ALFRED A. KNOPF

This is a work of fiction. Names, characters, places, and incidents either are the product of the author's imagination
or are used fictitiously. Any resemblance to actual persons, living or dead, events, or locales is entirely coincidental.

Copyright © 2012 by Maxwell Eaton III

All rights reserved. Published in the United States by Alfred A. Knopf, an imprint of Random House Children's Books, a division of
Random House, Inc., New York. Knopf, Borzoi Books, and the colophon are registered trademarks of Random House, Inc.

Visit us on the Web! www.randomhouse.com/kids

Educators and librarians, for a variety of teaching tools, visit us at www.randomhouse.com/teachers

Library of Congress Cataloging-in-Publication Data

Eaton, Maxwell.

The flying beaver brothers and the evil penguin plan / Maxwell Eaton III. — 1st ed.

p.   cm.

Summary: Two beavers thwart an evil plot by penguins, who plan to turn Beaver Island into a frosty resort.

ISBN 978-0-375-86447-6 (pbk.) — ISBN 978-0-375-96447-3 (lib. bdg.)

[1. Beavers—Fiction. 2. Penguins—Fiction. 3. Islands—Fiction.] I. Title.

PZ7.E3892Fly 2012   [E]—dc22   2010050652

The illustrations in this book were created using pen and ink with digital coloring.

MANUFACTURED IN MALAYSIA   January 2012   10 9 8 7 6 5 4 3 2 1   First Edition

Random House Children's Books supports the First Amendment and celebrates the right to read.

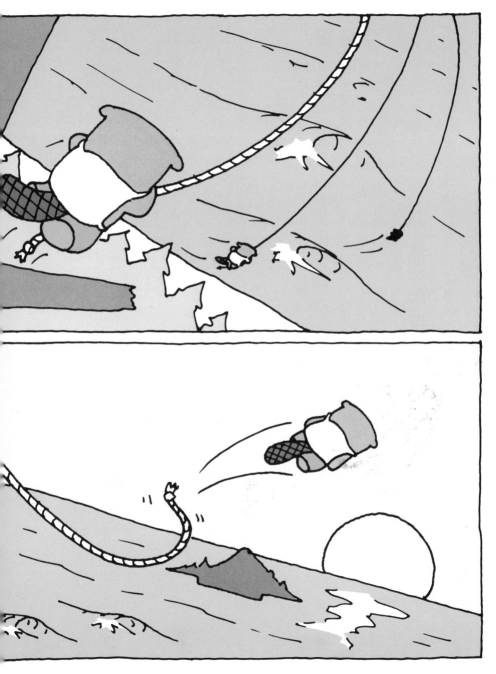

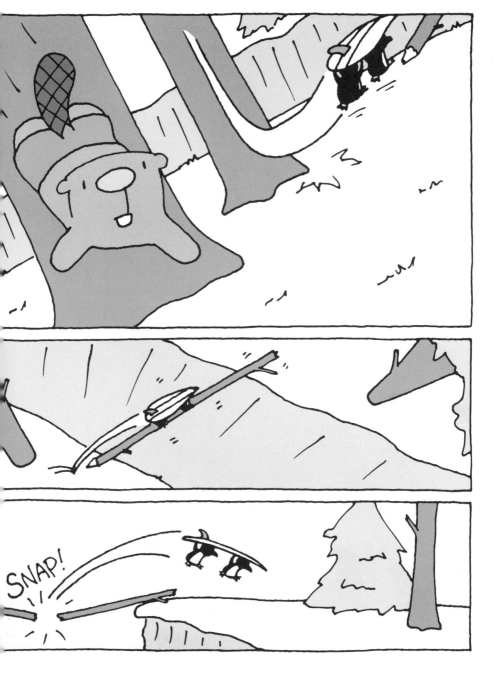

SNAP!

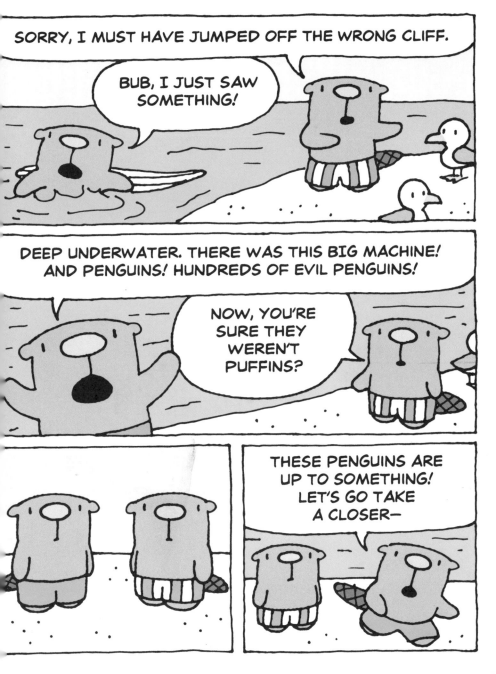

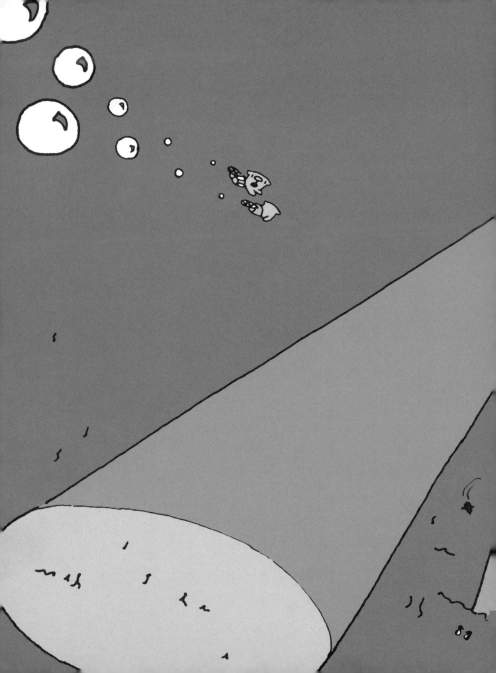

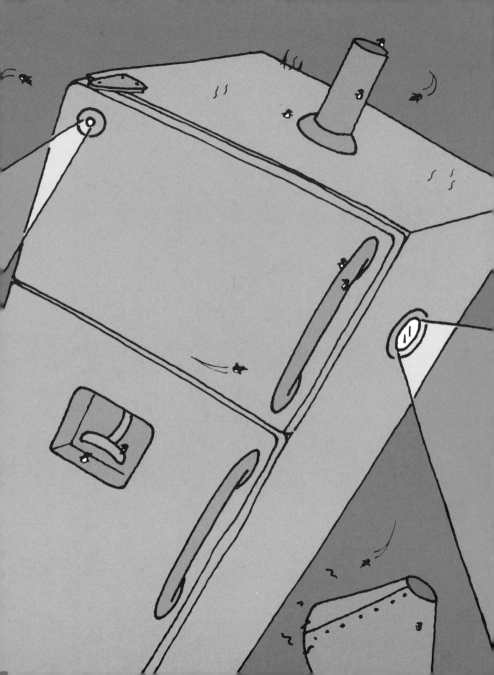

SO HOW ARE WE SUPPOSED TO GET INSIDE THIS MACHINE?

CLICK

I THINK I SAW A LITTLE DOOR DOWN THERE. HERE, I'LL DRAW IT FOR YOU....

BLUEPRINTS, EH? MUST BE A SECRET PLAN TO HELP ACE WIN THE SURFING COMPETITION. A SECRET PLAN TO MAKE ME LOSE!

BUT THE BRUCE DON'T LOSE!

LUCKILY, I'VE GOT JUST THE THING TO *CATCH* ME THE TROPHY TOMORROW.

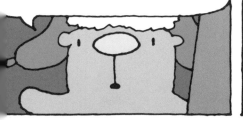

AND BY *CATCH* I MEAN PUT A NET IN THE WATER TO SNAG ACE'S BOARD SO THAT HE CAN'T WIN.

MUAHAHAHAHA!

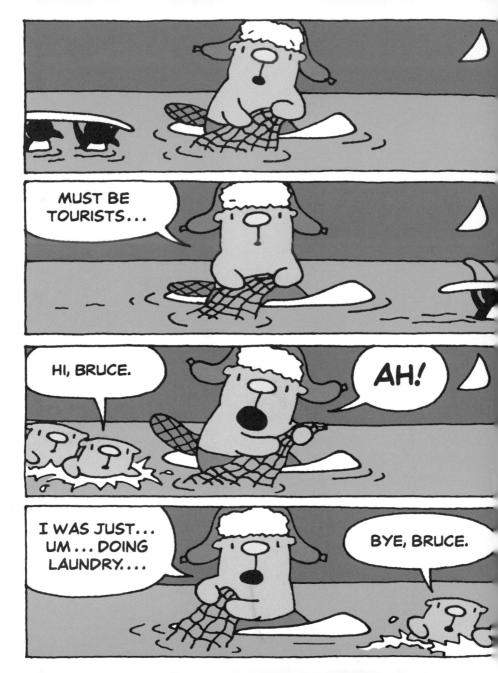

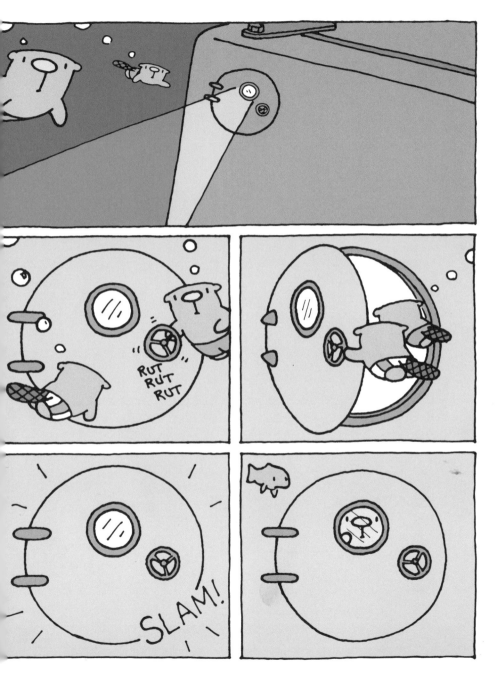

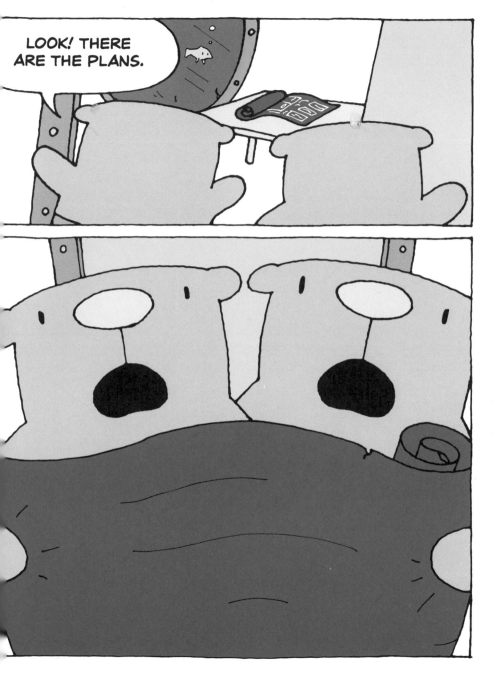

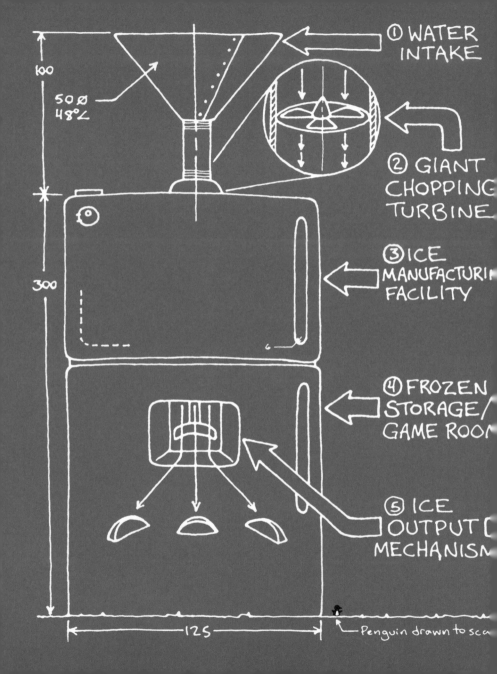

① WATER
INTAKE

② GIANT
CHOPPING
TURBINE

③ ICE
MANUFACTURI
FACILITY

④ FROZEN
STORAGE/
GAME ROO

⑤ ICE
OUTPUT
MECHANISM

100

50 Ø
48°∠

300

125

Penguin drawn to sca

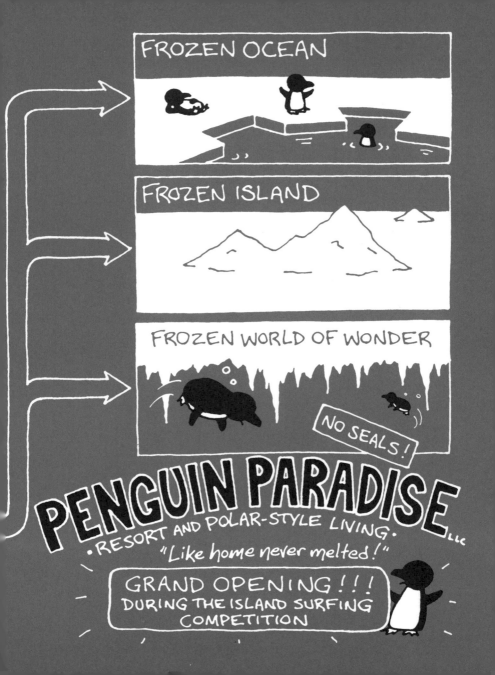

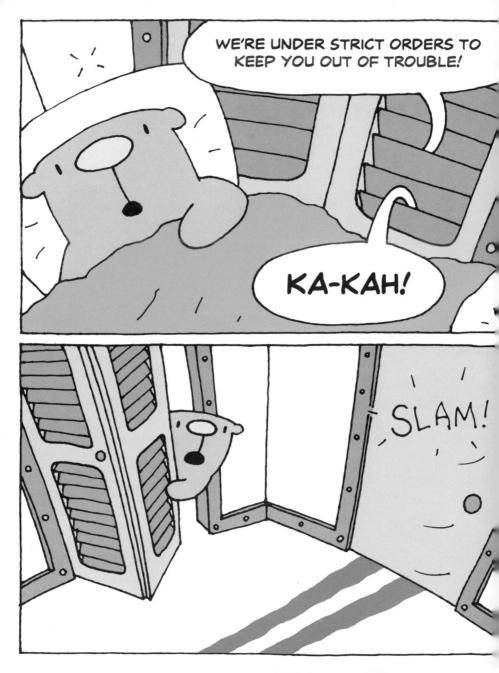

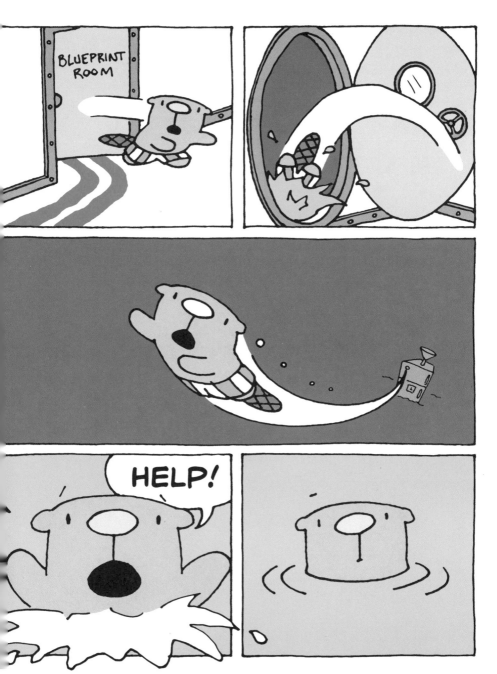

WITHDRAWN